W9-DET-118

Kids in Their Communities™

I Live on a Farm

Stasia Ward Kehoe

The Rosen Publishing Group's

PowerKids Press™

New York

For Kevin, Thomas, and Mak

Published in 2000 by The Rosen Publishing Group, Inc.
29 East 21st Street, New York, NY 10010

First Edition

Book Design: Michael de Guzman

Photo Illustrations by Christine Innamorato

Kehoe, Stasia Ward, 1968–
  I live on a farm / Stasia Ward Kehoe.
     p. cm. —(Kids in their communities)
  Summary: A seven-year-old boy who lives on a farm in upstate New York describes life in that rural community including the various kinds of work done during each season.
  ISBN 0-8239-5438-2
  1. Farm life—New York (State)—Red Hook Juvenile literature. 2. Rural children—New York (State)—Red Hook—Juvenile literature. 3. Community life—New York (State)—Red Hook—Juvenile literature. 4. Red Hook (N.Y.)—Rural conditions Juvenile literature. 5. Red Hook (N.Y.)—Social life and customs Juvenile literature. [1. Farm customs.] I. Title. II. Series: Kehoe, Stasia Ward, 1968– Kids in their communities.
HT442.R44K44 1999
307.72'09747'23—dc21   99-26372
                          CIP

Manufactured in the United States of America

CONTENTS

Robinson

My name is Robinson. I am seven years old. I live on a farm. Our farm is near the Hudson River in Dutchess County, New York. There are more than 600 farms in Dutchess County. There are 60 farms in my town of Red Hook alone. Everything from carrots and cabbages to peaches and plums are grown here. Mom says people call Red Hook the "Bread Basket of the Hudson Valley" because so much food comes from our town.

◀ *Here's me with one of my favorite four-footed friends!*

My Farm

On our 500-acre farm, we grow asparagus, peas, pumpkins, apples, flowers, berries, corn, and hay. We also raise cows. We have two big barns, three **storage silos**, a market building, a greenhouse, a garden shop, and many fields.

I can see our farm buildings, like the store that you see here, from my bedroom window.

Farm Family

It takes a lot of people to run a farm. Paul, the **herdsman**, has been taking care of our cows for 35 years. Our field **manager**, Gareth, plows the fields and fixes the tractors. Julie is in charge of running the market. Other people work here for just part of the year. During the fall **harvest**, more than 80 people work on our farm.

 Gareth rides this tractor around the fields.

A Cycle of Seasons

Each season on a farm brings its own special jobs. In the winter, we **prune** our fruit trees and bushes. Pruning them means cutting back all of the long branches and vines so that new fruit will be big and easy to pick. In the spring, we plow the fields to make the ground soft. Then we sow, or plant, the seeds. All summer, we hoe and **cultivate** the fields to keep them free from weeds. Long **irrigation** pipes set in the fields are used to water the plants.

Someday I want to learn how to drive the tractor myself. ▶

Harvest Festival

I love fall on the farm. We have a big Harvest Festival every year. There are bands playing, good foods to eat, and **mazes** to run through. The mazes are made out of corn and **bales** of hay. Lots of people come to see our farm and shop in the market during the Harvest Festival. I collect tickets at the start of the hay maze. I like to watch all the fun.

 We use bales of hay, like the one I'm sitting on, to make the hay maze.

13

Good Growing

To have a good harvest, you need to take care of your land. Each year we **rotate** our crops. Instead of planting corn in the same field every year, we might plant corn there one year and peas there the next. This helps to keep the soil healthy. We do not spray many **chemicals** on our plants to keep bad bugs away. Dad brings in **predator** insects. These are good bugs that eat the bad bugs so that the plants can grow big and strong.

In the winter the fields look quiet, but they will be busy again in the spring. ▶

Farmers in Red Hook

Many years ago, all of the activities in Red Hook were organized to help out the farmers. Stores were opened early in the morning, so farmers could shop before they began their chores. Schools were closed during busy planting and harvest seasons so children could help out in the fields. Today, Red Hook is like most other towns. Life is not organized around farming anymore, but we are still proud of our many beautiful farms and hardworking farmers.

 I like to help out at our store when I can.

School

   I am in the second grade at my school. Most of my friends don't live on farms, so they were excited to visit my farm this year. We gave my class a hayride to the farm. They enjoyed seeing the beautiful fish in our pond and visiting the animals in the petting zoo. We brought lots of corn back to school for a **cornhusking** contest. My classmates raced to see who could remove the outer leaves, or husks, from the corncobs the fastest.

Our animals have lots of visitors so they are not shy. ▶

Where Does the Food Go?

I told my friends that we call the asparagus, apples, corn, and other foods we grow **produce**. They wanted to know where all the produce goes after it is harvested. The answer is that it goes a lot of places! People can buy fruits and vegetables at our market, or pick their own from our fields. Some produce goes to restaurants. **Wholesalers** buy some of our produce to send to grocery stores across the country. We eat some of the food at our own house!

◀ *We make jams and jellies from the fruit we grow.*

Farm Life

My grandparents bought this farm in 1942. Grammy and Grandpa worked hard on the farm. They planted crops and raised dairy cows for milk. Today, fewer and fewer people live on farms. It is harder than ever to make money on a family farm. The farm is changing, but it is still a great place to live. I hope I always live on a farm. Mom says we'll take it one year at a time.

Glossary

bales (BAYLZ) Square blocks of hay or straw tied together.

chemicals (KEH-mih-kulz) Substances used to cause reactions.

cornhusking (KORN-hus-kyng) To remove outer leaves, or husks, from corn.

cultivate (KUL-tih-vayt) To prepare ground for growing crops.

harvest (HAR-vist) A season's gathered crop.

herdsman (HURDZ-min) One who keeps track of a farm's cows.

irrigation (ih-rih-GAY-shun) To carry water to land through pipes.

manager (MA-nih-jur) A person who directs others in their work.

mazes (MAYZ-es) Confusing passages that people try to find their way through in a game.

predator (PREH-duh-ter) An animal that kills other animals to eat.

produce (PRUH-doos) Fruits and vegetables.

prune (PROON) To cut off, or cut back, to help something grow.

rotate (ROH-tayt) To alternate or switch.

storage silos (STOR-ij SI-lowz) Tube-shaped, airtight structures.

wholesaler (HOL-say-lur) A person who sells goods that someone else has produced.

Index

Web Site:

To learn more about farms:
http://www.ffa.org/